Dear Parent:

Congratulations! Your child is taking the first steps on an exciting journey. The destination? Independent reading!

STEP INTO READING® will help your child get there. The program offers five steps to reading success. Each step includes fun stories and colorful art. There are also Step into Reading Sticker Books, Step into Reading Math Readers, Step into Reading Phonics Readers, Step into Reading Write-In Readers, and Step into Reading Phonics Boxed Sets—a complete literacy program with something to interest every child.

Learning to Read, Step by Step!

Ready to Read   Preschool–Kindergarten
• big type and easy words • rhyme and rhythm • picture clues
For children who know the alphabet and are eager to begin reading.

Reading with Help   Preschool–Grade 1
• basic vocabulary • short sentences • simple stories
For children who recognize familiar words and sound out new words with help.

Reading on Your Own   Grades 1–3
• engaging characters • easy-to-follow plots • popular topics
For children who are ready to read on their own.

Reading Paragraphs   Grades 2–3
• challenging vocabulary • short paragraphs • exciting stories
For newly independent readers who read simple sentences with confidence.

Ready for Chapters   Grades 2–4
• chapters • longer paragraphs • full-color art
For children who want to take the plunge into chapter books but still like colorful pictures.

STEP INTO READING® is designed to give every child a successful reading experience. The grade levels are only guides. Children can progress through the steps at their own speed, developing confidence in their reading, no matter what their grade.

Remember, a lifetime love of reading starts with a single step!

To the students
of Montclair
Elementary School
—J.L.W.

Visit us on the Web!
StepIntoReading.com
randomhouse.com/kids

Educators and librarians, for a variety of teaching tools, visit us at randomhouse.com/teachers

ISBN: 978-0-7364-2884-2 (trade) — ISBN: 978-0-7364-8111-3 (lib. bdg.)
Printed in the United States of America   10 9 8 7 6 5 4 3 2 1

STEP INTO READING®

STEP 2

DISNEY · PIXAR

TOY STORY

Christmas Toys

By Jennifer Liberts Weinberg

Illustrated by the Disney Storybook Artists

Random House 🏠 New York

Andy plays
with Buzz Lightyear
and Sheriff Woody.

They are

his favorite toys.

Andy's mom
has a surprise.
They are going
on a trip for Christmas!
Andy is happy.
But he cannot
bring his toys.

Woody is sad.

He will miss Andy.

Rex and Buzz want
to cheer Woody up.

Bo Peep and her sheep
want to help.

Buzz wants

to give Woody

a <u>toy</u> Christmas!

Buzz brings
the toys together.
They make a plan.

They collect supplies.
They will give Woody
a merry Christmas!

Buzz, Jessie, and Bo Peep
wrap presents.
Rex and Hamm
put the presents
under the tree.

The Green Army Men
and the Aliens
add ribbons and bows.

Jessie makes
a Santa hat
for Rex.

Buzz makes Rex a beard.
The Green Army Men
turn RC into a sled.

It is Christmas Eve.

Woody still misses Andy.

Buzz tells Woody
that his friends have
a Christmas surprise!

Slinky shows Woody
a Christmas tree
made of cotton balls!
The Aliens
hang buttons.
The Green Army Men
make snowflakes
out of jacks.

Wheezy sings
Christmas carols
to Woody.

Jessie ties bows.
She hangs them
on the mantel.

Bo Peep reads
a Christmas story
to the toys.

The toys gather
by the Christmas tree.

Buzz makes
a light show
with his laser beam!
The toys cheer.
It is Christmas magic!

Rex and RC are ready

to give out the presents!

Jessie gives Hamm
a shiny quarter.
Hamm gives Jessie
a doll's dress.
Bo Peep gives Woody
a Christmas kiss.

The toys gather
around the tree.
They sing carols.

Woody is happy
to spend Christmas
with his friends.
He wishes them all
a merry Christmas.

The toys look
out the window.
Snow!
It is good to be
with friends
on Christmas!